1⁵

The Grinny Granny Donkey

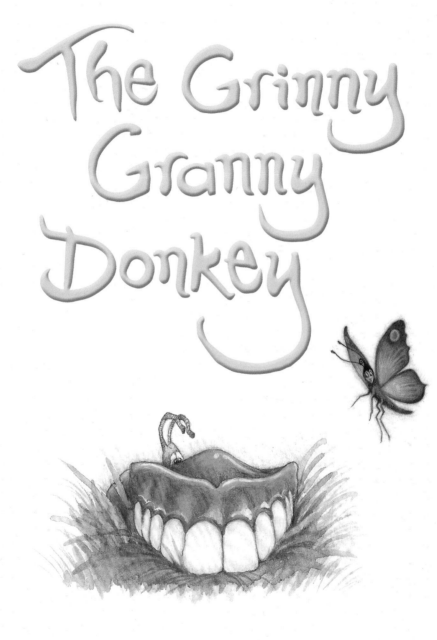

For Fiona, Archer and the original Grinny Granny herself,
Janice Clark. You will forever make me smile.
And for all the grandparents who sing and read to their grandchildren.
– Craig Smith

To Archer, may you always be filled with endless love and giggles,
and may you never forget that you have a marvellously magical
Scottish Granny who has melted hearts all over the world.
– Katz Cowley

This edition published in the UK in 2020 by Scholastic Children's Books
Euston House, 24 Eversholt Street, London NW1 1DB
A division of Scholastic Ltd
www.scholastic.co.uk
London – New York – Toronto – Sydney – Auckland – Mexico City – New Delhi – Hong Kong

First published in 2020 by Scholastic New Zealand Limited
Text © Craig Smith, 2020
Illustrations © Katz Cowley, 2020
The moral rights of Craig Smith and Katz Cowley have been asserted.

ISBN 978 0 702 30427 9

The Grinny Granny Donkey

Words by Craig Smith

Illustrations by Katz Cowley

■ SCHOLASTIC

There was a sweet donkey
who lived on the heath.

She was so funny
with her false teeth ...

Hee Haw!

But her teeth kept falling out!

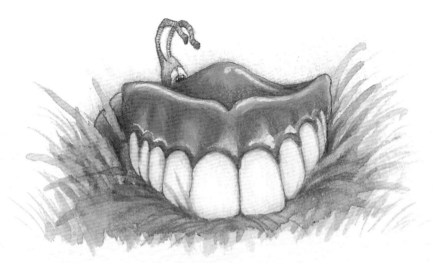

She was a
clunky donkey.

There was a sweet donkey who lived on the heath.
She was so funny with her false teeth ...

Hee Haw!

But her teeth kept falling out!

She loved to sip her favourite brew
and dunk her biscuits in it.

She was a
dunky-drinky,
clunky donkey.

There was a sweet donkey who lived on the heath.
She was so funny with her false teeth ...

Hee Haw!

But her teeth kept falling out!

She loved to sip her favourite brew,
dunk her biscuits in it ...

and fall asleep in the afternoon sun.

She was a **zonky**,
dunky-drinky,
clunky donkey.

There was a sweet donkey who lived on the heath.
She was so funny with her false teeth ...

Hee Haw!

But her teeth kept falling out!

She loved to sip her favourite brew,
dunk her biscuits in it,
fall asleep in the afternoon sun ...

then go for walks with her jewellery on.

She was a **clinky-clanky**, zonky, dunky-drinky, clunky donkey.

There was a sweet donkey who lived on the heath.
She was so funny with her false teeth …

Hee Haw!

But her teeth kept falling out!

She loved to sip her favourite brew,
dunk her biscuits in it,
fall asleep in the afternoon sun,
go for walks with her jewellery on …

and she always dressed smartly.

She was a **swanky**,
clinky-clanky, zonky,
dunky-drinky,
clunky donkey.

There was a sweet donkey who lived on the heath.
She was so funny with her false teeth ...

Hee Haw!

But her teeth kept falling out!

She loved to sip her favourite brew,
dunk her biscuits in it,
fall asleep in the afternoon sun,
go for walks with her jewellery on,
dress smartly ...

and she played her banjo to relax.

She was a
plunky-plinky,
swanky,
clinky-clanky,
zonky,
dunky-drinky,
clunky donkey.

There was a sweet donkey who lived on the heath.
She was so funny with her false teeth ...

Hee Haw!

But her teeth kept falling out!

She loved to sip her favourite brew,
dunk her biscuits in it,
fall asleep in the afternoon sun,
go for walks with her jewellery on,
dress smartly and play her banjo to relax ...

BUT if she hadn't had a visit from her family
in a while, she would sometimes get grumpy and cranky!

She was a **granky**,
plunky-plinky,
swanky,
clinky-clanky,
zonky,
dunky-drinky,
clunky donkey.

There was a sweet donkey who lived on the heath.
She was so funny with her false teeth ...

Hee Haw!

But her teeth kept falling out!

She loved to sip her favourite brew, dunk her biscuits in it,
fall asleep in the afternoon sun, go for walks with her
jewellery on, dress smartly, play her banjo to relax,
and sometimes she got grumpy and cranky ...

BUT when her son Wonky turned up with her cute
granddaughter Dinky, that granky granny donkey got
so many cuddles and kisses that she couldn't get the
smile off her face for weeks!

She was a **grinny granny**, plunky-plinky, swanky, clinky-clanky, zonky, dunky-drinky, clunky donkey.

There was a GRINNY GRANNY
donkey who lived on the heath.
She smiled so much you could
see her false teeth ...